Star Crossed at Twilight

A Scottish Regency Novella

REGENCY HISTORICALS
BY JOANNA MAITLAND

Unsuitable Matches Series
A Penniless Prospect
Marrying the Major
Rake's Reward

Star Crossed Lovers
My Lady Angel
Bride of the Solway
Star Crossed at Twilight*

The Aikenhead Honours
His Cavalry Lady
His Reluctant Mistress
His Forbidden Liaison
His Silken Seduction*

Individual Stories
A Poor Relation
The Earl's Mistletoe Bride

A Regency Invitation
[with Nicola Cornick & Elizabeth Rolls]

*published by Joanna Maitland Independent

Star Crossed at Twilight

A Scottish Regency Novella

JOANNA MAITLAND

Published in the United Kingdom
by Joanna Maitland Independent
http://libertabooks.com

Star Crossed At Twilight
a retitled and revised edition of the ebook novella
originally published under the title Delight and Desire in 2010
by Harlequin Mills & Boon Ltd by arrangement with
Harlequin Books S.A.

ISBN: 978-0-9957046-3-3

This book is a work of fiction. Names, characters, places and
incidents are the product of the author's imagination or have
been used fictitiously and are not to be construed as real. Any
resemblance to actual persons, living or dead, or to events or
places, is entirely coincidental.

Cover Design and Interior Formatting: Joanna Maitland
Cover Images: Bigstock.com/Faux Toe and Joanna Maitland

DEDICATION

This first print edition is dedicated to those
readers who loved *Bride of the Solway*,
the full-length novel in which Robert and
Isobel first appeared, but who were unable to
read my star crossed lovers' story because it
was only available as an ebook.
I hope it has been worth the wait.

CONTENTS

CHAPTER ONE

Scotland, Spring 1800

THE LIGHT AND THE PLACE WERE magical, as ever. As was the silence. Soon the twilight would come, to make everything perfect.

Major Robert Anstruther tethered his horse and started towards the castle. Here, at Caerlaverock, he could be alone, to reflect on his future in the enfolding tranquillity of the moated ruin.

He paused a moment to gaze up at the castle's stout gate towers, their red colour deepening in the first rays of the setting sun. How many marauding armies had been repulsed from here, in the centuries when

Scotland and England were separate, warring kingdoms? Nowadays, the kingdoms were joined and at peace, at least with one another. Wars were fought overseas.

As if to remind him of his own role in those wars, a sharp twinge of pain lanced through his injured leg. He muttered an oath and shifted his weight. He had expected to be fully fit again by now, and able to rejoin his regiment, but it would take some time yet. He grimaced. His army career must take second place for now, since his poor father could not survive much longer after that last seizure. Robert, as the only son, had had to promise to set about finding himself a wife.

In the gathering dusk, the mist was rising from the moat, starting to shroud Caerlaverock as if to hide it from prying eyes, like some fairytale castle. Such a magic and mysterious place should be home to the ghosts of ancient warriors, cut down in bloody battle, or perhaps to nymphs and naiads, rising from the watery depths, their golden curls glistening.

Robert began to stroll towards the gate, musing on those strange thoughts. In all the years he had been coming here, in the twilight of dawn or dusk, he had never once met another human being. Nor a spirit, either. If they were here, they kept themselves well hidden.

Perhaps things had changed since his last visit, years ago? He had been out of the country a long time. He fancied that Caerlaverock was eternal, though. Its serene beauty never changed.

He had just crossed the moat on the rickety makeshift bridge and was going down into the dark narrows between the gate towers when he heard it – a silvery, tinkling laugh, floating on the drift of mist rising from the rushes. Some nymph *was* here, it seemed. And she had awakened just in time for the twilight that Robert so loved.

Intrigued, Robert crept down the stone passage, straining eyes and ears for any clue to where his nymph might be. Logic told him that he had imagined the sound, that there could not possibly be any fairy woman here, no matter how magical these ruins might seem. And yet he found himself putting one foot softly and warily in front of the other, in case a crunch of gravel should scare her away. If she was here, he wanted to see her, to touch her, before she melted back into the silent waters of the moat.

Another sound, carried on the mist. Not a laugh this time, but a song, a female voice humming a low, mysterious melody. It spoke wordlessly of lost love and heartbreak. Local legend said a water nymph would always mourn the love she could not have. But if an earthly man could kiss her, the nymph would be anchored to the human world for ever, and in thrall to the man who had shown her what human love could be.

Robert shook his head against his own fanciful imaginings, but he still crept silently forward to reach the open courtyard, beyond the gloom of the passage. He had to know.

She *was* there. High up on the battlements,

3

on top of the tower, surrounded by mist, she seemed to be dancing on the air. It was difficult to see her clearly against the rays of the setting sun, but he had an impression of naked limbs clad in a damply clinging gown of filmy white, and a mane of red-gold hair hanging in loose curls around bare shoulders, glinting as it caught the dying light. She was dancing back and forth, weightless and floating, her naked arms raised towards the sunset.

She could not be real. But even so, no man could see such a vision without wishing to possess it. That seductive voice was luring him on, catching at all his senses. She must not be allowed to dissolve back into the mist. A water maiden's kiss must surely be worth any risk? Kissing her, embracing her – would it be like trying to catch flowing water, impossible to hold, and as elusive as quicksilver?

Keeping to the shadows, he circled the courtyard until he came to the tower. He could hear her still, but she was hidden from him now by the vast bulk of the stonework. He crept up the spiral stairs, his eyes wide against the gloom, his ears attuned to the floating notes of her melody. The pain of his injury was pushed aside in his heart-thumping eagerness to reach the top, to snatch his prize. When he emerged, would she be gone? No, he could still hear her voice, drifting on the mist-laden air in long watery notes, sometimes so soft they might be no more than a breeze from the estuary and the sea beyond.

But there was no breeze. The evening was totally still. Only the rising mist was moving, to protect the ruin from mortal eyes while its queen, this beautiful nymph, ascended her battlement throne. If he could capture her...

The light was just above him. He was about to emerge. He pressed his body against the wall of the staircase and stopped to listen. She sounded very near. He risked a rapid glance round the stonework and only just managed to swallow the gasp that rose in his throat.

She *was* there! A beautiful illusion, perhaps, but almost near enough to touch.

She was smiling rather wistfully, humming still, and her eyes were closed. Her face was lifted towards the west. In the low sunshine, her curls were glowing like a fiery halo around her head. She seemed to be dancing with some invisible cavalier, holding out one long slim arm as if waiting for her partner to take it and kiss her hand.

It was an invitation no man could resist. Robert stepped out into the light, clasped her outstretched fingers and pulled her into his arms, eager yet dreading the inevitable moment of loss when she faded into chilly, watery nothingness.

But she was not cold. Nor was she light as thistledown, like the fairies of his childhood tales. His nymph was cool and almost alive, as if she were already halfway to the earthly reality that he could offer her with his kiss, and with his body.

He drew her closer and stroked a hand over her flowing hair, letting its silken strands caress his palm. Her magic was already possessing him totally. And he must possess her in turn.

His pulse was racing. His whole body was a mass of surging heat and desire. Yet his first kiss was gentle, hesitant, the merest touch on a mouth that was cool and unresponsive. Nymph-like, she was not ready to yield.

But neither did she pull away.

It was enough. Now he began to kiss her in earnest, with only one insistent thought hammering through the raging chaos of his mind. If he could make his nymph respond to him, she would be earthbound, and his, for ever.

As the kiss continued, less gently now, he felt slim arms glide round his neck, touching his skin, his hair. He was making her ever more real. He would make her his. If he wanted to hold her, he must make love to her. But not by force. She could still flee, still melt into the mist. She must be made to want him, to long for him as he was now longing for her.

Greatly daring, he touched the very tip of his tongue to the middle of her lower lip. He felt the sweet breath of her sigh against his skin as she opened to him. It was a magical sound, as if all the notes of her fairy song had been combined in a single radiant chord. It was an invitation. And a promise.

Gently at first, he began running his tongue along the length of her lips, touching and withdrawing, then kissing teasingly at the corners of her mouth, challenging her to respond. He was not mistaken in her. She drew him closer and pulled his head down towards her so that she could begin to kiss him back, following his every move. She touched her tongue to his lower lip, just as he had done, waiting for his answering sigh. She caressed his lips, as he had done, and touched a featherlight kiss to each corner of his mouth.

It seemed that she could follow, and willingly, but she would not lead.

With a groan he could not suppress, Robert began to deepen their magical kiss. His nymph was weaving an enchantment around him, capturing him as he had hoped to capture her. He did not care. Every fibre of his being longed for her.

He drew her closer still and touched his tongue to the tip of hers, tasting the honeyed sweetness of her mouth. In an instant, she was responding, their tongues twining, demanding, seeking each other in an ancient dance of love. One light hand moved to touch his cheek, stroking down to his jaw, then lifted again to thread itself into his hair.

He held her now. She would truly be his. He slid his fingers down the length of her upraised arm, caressing her bare shoulder, her neck, the silky skin of her upper back. He could feel the edge of her gown, so light and thin that it seemed to be made of gossamer. She ought to have wings, but she did not. And soon she would be truly earthbound.

He stroked the back of his fingers down the side of her neck, across her throat to the curve of her upper breast. So beautiful, so tempting. For a second, he cupped one breast in his hand, delighting in its weight. She was almost real, almost human now. He could feel her nipple rising against his palm. He deepened the kiss yet more and began to push aside her flimsy bodice.

"No!"

A single word, full of fear. It struck him like a lightning bolt.

In that same instant, Robert stepped away from her. His illusion shimmered and shredded and was gone.

He looked.

What madness had been upon him? How could he ever have thought this living, breathing girl was anything but real? And he had been about to—

Self-loathing filled him. He could not look her in the face. He must be bright scarlet, or ashen. And she—?

Isobel spun away from him, her hands to her burning cheeks. She had— Oh, heavens, she had let herself be kissed by a complete stranger, and she had melted into him, returning his embraces as if she knew him, and trusted him, and wanted him... It was shameless, even more shameless than indulging the last dream of her girlhood by dancing here, alone in the sunset, in a borrowed, forbidden gown.

She shivered. Was that the dampened muslin clinging to her skin? Or was it his presence, this unknown man who had walked into her dream as if he belonged there, as if he were meant to share it?

Behind her, there was no sound. No

movement. If he was simply a character in her fantasy, he must surely have vanished into the mist? Yet his scent lingered around her still – wool, and leather, and living, breathing man. That alone should be enough to terrify a vulnerable woman.

But it did not. Her body was glowing, inside and out. It wanted to return to his embrace as if they belonged together.

The silence lengthened. The mist was thickening more quickly now, starting to block out the last rays of the darkening sun. Soon it would drop below the horizon and the twilight proper would come, the magical twilight that so enchanted these ruins.

Would he still be there, reaching out to her, if she turned to him in the gathering dusk? Or had she imagined it all?

She forced her hands to her sides, took a deep breath and turned.

He was still there.

"You *are* real," she whispered hoarsely.

His gaze was fixed on her face. His mouth twisted slowly into a half-smile. "And so are you."

He had not moved even an inch. It was as if her spoken refusal of him had turned his tall lean frame to marble. It seemed that only his mouth could move. It was a mouth made for smiling, and for kissing…

She dropped her gaze. Her heart was pounding all over again, and even faster now. Surely he could hear it?

She took a deep breath and raised her chin a little, though her gaze remained fixed on the stones at her feet. "Sir, I—"

"Miss Isobel! Where are you?"

Isobel gasped in horror at the sound of that distant voice. "My maid! She has returned to fetch me."

She glanced down at her borrowed gown, seeing it now as he must have seen it – damp, flimsy, revealing the body beneath as if she were naked. "She must not see me dressed in this."

"She must not see you alone with me, either."

His tone was such an odd mixture of grave concern and suppressed humour that she risked a glance up into his face. His mouth was stern, but she was certain – almost certain – that there was a hint of mischief in his hooded eyes. The desire that had sparked between them seemed to have melted away like Caerlaverock mist.

For now.

"Where are your clothes?" His voice had turned sharp, and commanding.

She realised, for the first time, that he was a military man, dressed in full regimentals. She pointed a shaky finger to the heap of clothing by the wall, the heavy gown she had discarded in order to discover, just once, how it would feel to be clad in the skimpy muslins that were forbidden to her. Indecent, her father called them. And, wearing them, her behaviour had been indecent, too.

"I will go down the stairs so that you may change in private. Make haste." He started for the dark entrance to the staircase.

"No, do not go down! She must not see you."

He turned back, smiling reassuringly. "She will not. I shall go down only far enough to ensure your modesty. When you are ready, and presentable again, you may come down by yourself. There will be room to pass. I promise – on my honour – that I will not attack you again." His smile disappeared when he spoke those words and he shook his head, as if trying to be rid of an unwelcome thought.

He was an honourable man. She knew that, in spite of the madness that had possessed them both. And now he was behaving with more restraint than Isobel deserved.

"Miss Isobel?" It was Annie's worried voice.

Isobel crossed to the battlement where it overlooked the courtyard. She leant over, allowing only her head to show. "I am up here on the tower, Annie, watching the sunset. Gather up my painting things and take them out to the carriage, if you please. I shall be down in a few moments."

From the shadow of the doorway, he smiled and nodded approvingly at her. He was about to leave. They would pass just once more in the darkness, in silence, and she would never see him again.

She started to reach out a hand, but then let it drop to her side. "Sir, I— You must allow me to thank you, and to explain..." Her voice, never more than a whisper at best, faltered into nothing. She felt lost.

His smile widened the merest fraction. "I will come again tomorrow, at dusk, in hopes of seeing an enchanting vision once more.

11

Tomorrow, and every day after, just in case..."
He let the promise hang in the air. Then,
without another word, he disappeared into the
darkness.

He took two steps down, stopping to lean
his forehead against the cold stone wall,
waiting for his heart to slow and for his eyes to
become accustomed to the gloom. Behind him,
on the stone platform, he could hear the sound
of clothing being shaken out, and quick
nervous breathing as she grappled with tapes
and pins. He must not stay here, picturing her
transformation from nymph to earthbound
lady. He did not want to be seduced by that.
He wanted to remember her as he had first
seen her – ethereal, floating, fairylike.

He moved a little further from the light. He
was beginning to see the shapes of walls and
steps now. And he was almost back in control.
It was safe to move. He started down the
staircase, resolutely ignoring the ache in his
leg. It had returned to remind him of his
mortality. And, indirectly, of hers. He must not
dwell on that. More important to concentrate
on muffling the sound of his leather boots on
the stones. The abigail below must hear
nothing.

Halfway down, Robert stopped and shrank
back against the wall at the narrow end of the
steps so that there would be room enough for
her to pass without touching him. He was in
the darkest part of the staircase, too dark to see
her in her everyday garb. Would she know he
was there? He was resolved not to betray his
presence by word or movement. It must be as

if he had become part of these cold blank stones.

He heard a step then, far above. She was wearing quite heavy shoes, or perhaps even boots. On the battlements, he had fancied her feet were bare.

He strained his ears, listening for her approach. For a moment there was nothing. She was probably waiting, as he had done, until she could see her way in the darkness. Then he heard light steps on the stairs, coming ever closer, and the soft shush of heavy fabric brushing across the edges of the stones.

He held his breath, waiting. She was very close now.

It was the scent that reached him first. Lavender, he was sure of it. And yet he had smelled no lavender when he held her in his arms. A heavy skirt brushed against his thigh, and the scent wafted up around him. It was not unpleasant, and yet it was not her. His nymph had smelled of watery magic, and then of desire, not of the lavender of common clothes presses.

She had stopped. She must sense that he was there, beside her.

He tried not to breathe, tried to ignore the alien scent from her gown.

The briefest touch on his fingers. Not silk, but warm living skin. She had caressed his hand.

"Tomorrow. Dusk," she whispered.

And then she was gone.

CHAPTER TWO

ISOBEL PAUSED, WATERCOLOUR BRUSH IN HAND.

It would soon be dusk. Would he keep his promise?

Her heart began to pound. It was madness. She should not have come. He was a gentleman. He would never accept Isobel as a lady. Not after what had passed between them on the top of that tower.

It was absurd to be waiting here, indulging her foolish dreams yet again. Yesterday she had worn that indecent chemise gown, dampening her muslin skirts in daring self-indulgence. She had even unpinned her hair and kicked off her shoes. She had thought herself totally alone, enacting her fantasy, her last moment of freedom before she had to give herself to duty and a loveless marriage. But then *he* had appeared, like a fairytale prince, taking her proffered hand and...

That kiss had been no fantasy. It had been delight, and desire. It had been glorious.

And utter wickedness.

She should leave here before he came, before it was too late. She must not meet him again. A woman of almost twenty could not afford to dally in the unattainable dreams of childhood.

She told herself sternly that she should be concentrating on the vital business of finding a rich husband. Otherwise, the Anstruthers would finally triumph in their ancient feud with her family. In previous centuries, many had died, on both sides of the Ritchie-Anstruther feud. Nowadays there was no more blood-letting; the weapons of choice were wealth and power. She, Isobel Lang Ritchie, was her family's last hope – she would have just this one London season – and if she failed, her family would soon be bankrupt.

With a shake of her head, she began to pack up her painting things. But then she paused again. *Slowly, Isobel. Enjoy the moment. This could be the last time you will be free to sit here on a spring evening, in the silence of the early dusk, feeling the pull of these crumbling, tight-lipped stones. They know your secrets, but they will not tell.*

You are safe here. He will not come.

Twisting tendrils of mist were beginning to climb the walls. With a sigh, Isobel rose to her feet and let her gaze roam the triangular courtyard. Very ghostly now, in the failing light. She could sense the same age-old magic that had gripped her yesterday.

Her heart began to beat a little faster.

And then she saw it. A watery outline, barely visible in the shadows of the gatehouse, like the ghost of some Caerlaverock defender, long dead, come to find her and bid her farewell.

He had come. He had kept his promise.

Tall and spare, he walked calmly out of the shadows until he was standing only feet from Isobel's frozen body. She could neither speak nor flee. She stared at him, as if seeing him for the first time. Regimentals, dark hair, a strong, lived-in face. Age impossible to determine, for war matured a man. Thirty, perhaps?

She felt a rustle of petticoats at her back. "Miss Isobel…"

Isobel hushed her old nurse with an impatient gesture. Her soldier was an honourable man. Had he not proved it just yesterday?

He bowed a little stiffly and spoke politely, as if to a chance-met stranger. "Forgive me, ma'am. I have intruded. I fear I— Perhaps you will permit me to introduce myself? Major Robert Anstruther. At your service."

Anstruther? Terror sliced through her gut and froze every muscle in her body. No, please, no!

She was ruined. She had behaved like a wanton with a man who was worse than a stranger – he was a mortal enemy. The

Anstruthers were devils – *every last one of them* – and all bent on completing the destruction of the Ritchies. Isobel had learned that from the cradle. And now she herself had handed him the weapon to strike her down.

She had thought Caerlaverock her protector. But the castle had played a cruel trick on her, drawing her into the arms of an enemy for her very first kiss.

This place was not enchanted; it was cursed. And so was she.

Behind her, Annie was sucking in a horrified breath. Isobel spun round to silence the woman before she could pronounce the fateful name of Ritchie. He must not learn her true name. That was her only chance of escape.

She must look him in the face, and lie.

She took a deep breath and turned back to him. She forced herself to ignore the fear pounding through her veins, and to smile serenely up at this Anstruther monster. "I am Isobel Lang, from Dumfries, sir." She curtsied politely.

"Delighted to make your acquaintance, Miss Lang." He bowed again and came forward, walking with a very slight limp. So he had been wounded in battle, serving his country. Could that redeem even an Anstruther?

No, he was still a monster. She must not allow herself to admire this man, or to think well of him in any way. He had the power to ruin her.

She must not let him see that she was afraid. She must do nothing to arouse his suspicions. Good manners, and innocuous conversation.

That was the only route to safety.

"Thank you, Major. I must tell you that we were on the point of leaving, so you do not intrude."

A startled expression crossed his face. Then he frowned. Had he expected her to remain with him, to continue what they had begun in the magic of yesterday's twilight? The very thought of that was bringing the heat to her cheeks. She must get away from this dangerous man.

His frown disappeared. She fancied he gave a tiny shrug. "You paint, ma'am?" He gestured towards Isobel's stool and sketch pad. "May I look?"

Isobel hesitated for only a second. He was simply being polite. Best to offer her work for a frank assessment, followed by a swift farewell. "I am afraid I have never yet succeeded in capturing the special quality of this place." She offered her pad. "As you will no doubt see."

He did her the courtesy of studying her work with care. "I am not sure that anyone ever could," he said thoughtfully. "Though I do think you have caught Murdoch's Tower extremely well. Solid and somehow ephemeral – magical – at the same time."

He smiled down at her then, in a dangerously beguiling way. The fear that was knotting her gut began to subside, overcome by the heat of invading memories. It was almost as if they were embracing through her painting. Touching each other all over again. Why did he have to mention Murdoch's Tower? The place where they had— Now

19

even her skin was beginning to burn.

"Thank you, sir," she replied quickly, trying to damp down her warring senses. Desperate not to betray herself further, she found herself stammering, "You... er... you know Caerlaverock well?"

He nodded. "I came here often when I was living at home. You will think me a strange kind of soldier, I fear, but I always used to come here at dawn or dusk. To enjoy the twilight solitude."

"Then we had best leave you at once, sir." She started to turn away.

He put out a hand. It stopped inches from her arm and yet she felt the crackle of awareness, as if they had touched, and held. "Ah, no, ma'am. Pray do not leave on my account."

There was a peculiar smile in his eyes as he looked at her, a mixture of understanding and...and intimacy. He was trying to help her through this encounter. But he wanted her to know that he remembered everything. And that she should remember, too.

Her body remembered all too well. There was now a molten, glowing core, deep in her belly, urging her to reach for him, to—

This was madness. She must be possessed to let down her guard with a sworn enemy. At that terrifying realisation, the glow in her belly turned instantly back to ice.

She closed her eyes for a second while she struggled with her fears.

From somewhere deep within, she found new strength. She would flatter him, and then outwit him.

He was politely ignoring her strained silence. "You have just as much right to enjoy this place as I do, ma'am. More, if you are going to paint it. I have no such talent to offer. All I can do is gaze around, and try to fix it in my memory." He glanced down at her sketch pad. "I wonder— But no. That would be an imposition."

She could end it. Now.

Without hesitation, she tore out the page. "It is a paltry attempt, sir, but if it may help you to remember a favourite place when you are serving far from home, I will give it willingly."

He accepted it as though it were a masterpiece, and priceless. For a moment, he stood staring down at it. Then he stowed it carefully inside his uniform jacket. "Thank you, Miss Lang. You are very generous."

"Miss Isobel. I can hear the carriage. We should leave."

Oh, heavens! She had forgotten that the carriage could betray her. What if he recognised it? He must not see it. She had to divert his attention, somehow.

Without pausing to think, she said quickly, "Would you be so good as to give me your escort, sir? I should welcome one last look across the moat before I go. Annie will take my painting things out to the carriage and return for me in just a moment."

Isobel's fierce look silenced Annie's protest. With amazing speed, the maid gathered up all their belongings and hurried out of the courtyard.

Isobel let him usher her across the courtyard to the walkway between the two huge towers that faced towards the Solway Firth, and England. With the mist rising, the castle was again an island of other-worldly tranquillity, cut off from the day-to-day tumult of feuds, and poverty, and marriages without love. Her fears receded, lulled by the enveloping twilight. They were alone together again, but the enchantment they had shared could not come again. Fairy-tale fantasies were for children. They never came true.

For several minutes, she forced herself to make light conversation about nothing very much. Prompted by polite questions, she spoke of her painting and of her delight in plants and gardens. Safe enough. And so much safer than allowing herself to dwell on how his lips had tasted hers and taught her to respond to him, with a knowledge and desire she had not known she possessed.

Annie's distant footsteps on the gravel cut through her beckoning fantasy. She must end this, and save herself. "Sir, may I ask a favour of you?" Without giving him time to reply, she whispered urgently, "May I ask you *not* to escort me to my carriage? My coachman, you see, is a dreadful mischief-maker. If you were to escort me out, he would certainly inform my papa of this…er…encounter."

She swallowed again, trying not to remember how that first encounter had been. Just yesterday.

There was so much understanding in the look he bestowed on her then, that she flushed scarlet with embarrassment. And returning fear. If he once discovered she was a Ritchie, he would lose every shred of sympathy for her plight.

"Miss Isobel. The carriage is waiting."

"Thank you, Annie. I will come at once." She curtsied demurely, holding her breath. Her heart was pounding. Would he do as she asked?

He smiled politely and bowed, without moving to close the space between them. "Forgive me if I do not escort you out, ma'am. I fear—" He gestured towards his injured leg and shrugged his shoulders, as if in apology.

"I should not dream of asking you to do so, sir. I will wish you good day now." She bowed her head and turned away before he could reply. Then she slipped her arm through her maid's, and hurried her towards the exit.

Today's encounter with one her family's sworn enemies must not be spoken of, not to anyone. And yesterday's encounter? That must remain a deep, deep secret, buried where even Isobel herself could not find it.

CHAPTER THREE

Y ET ANOTHER TEDIOUS BALL!

Robert sighed heavily, but turned back to the glass to finish fastening his dress uniform. He was not at all sure why he had accepted Mrs Rougely's invitation, for she did not move in the highest levels of society. He supposed he was bored.

Over these past weeks in London, he had discovered that the huge wealth of the Anstruther estates attracted every purse-pinched parent with a daughter to dispose of. He had met dozens of them. The pretty ones were empty-headed and vain; the more thoughtful ones were plain and humourless. Not one had a fraction of Isobel Lang's extraordinary qualities. Isobel Lang was passionate about life. One day, she would make some lucky man a passionate wife.

Not for the first time, he wished that he had not heeded her wishes. He had not watched her leave, nor followed her home. Admittedly, he had enquired after gentry families called Lang, but the only Langs in the area were tradesmen. So Isobel Lang was not a lady. And he was duty-bound to forget her.

He had tried, but the delicious image of Isobel Lang refused to leave him. He remembered her standing on the top of Murdoch's tower, her image fuzzy in the sunset with the red-gold light around her, and later, in the twilight, gleaming softly like a muted star. He remembered the feel of her in his arms, her kiss on his lips. That innocent kiss had touched him to the core. She had made his blood fizz and boil like shaken champagne. In his memory, she was radiantly beautiful, and so very desirable. She had all the qualities to make a man a splendid wife.

All except birth.

His beautiful nymph was forbidden to him. Let her remain a magical, unattainable dream.

Considering the early hour, the room was remarkably full, though no one was yet dancing. He paused in the doorway to take the measure of the place, and of the company.

And then he saw her. Isobel Lang was standing in the midst of a group of young men. Robert fancied he had met one or two of them before, but he was too focused on gazing at Isobel to recall their names. She had been beautiful at Caerlaverock, but in the latest London fashions, she was transformed. She looked utterly radiant in a simple ballgown of daffodil yellow over a white slip. Tiny jonquils were nestling in her red-gold curls. She wore no jewels at all, but she had no need of them. He found himself longing to stroke her lustrous, pearly skin.

He strolled over to the group surrounding her. The young men parted politely, though reluctantly, to make way for him. As Robert bowed to the company, one of them said, "Why, it's Major Anstruther. Welcome, sir. You won't remember, but I'm Digben. We met briefly at the shooting gallery last month. May I introduce you to—?"

Robert cut him off with a dismissive wave. "Thank you, Digben, but the lady and I are already acquainted. And I could tell from across the room that she needed rescuing from a horde of young rascals like you." He smiled amiably round at them. None of them would dare to contradict a man nearly ten years their senior.

He bowed to Isobel and held out his hand. It was a challenge. Their gazes locked. It was if they were totally alone. And remembering that first touch. "May I have the honour of this dance, ma'am?"

She had become as white as her slip. Was she afraid that he might speak of what had happened between them that first day? He realised with a start that she was no tradesman's daughter after all. She had been admitted to a society ball. She really did have a lady's reputation to lose.

He threw her a long, meaningful look. She had trusted him before. She must do so again.

Her courage was undimmed. With the briefest nod towards a turbanned old lady seated by the wall, she took a step forward and laid her fingers on Robert's open hand. Then she smiled serenely at the younger men and said, "You will excuse me, gentlemen? I think the music is about to begin."

He closed his fingers around hers and drew her arm through his. Despite layers of fabric, he could feel the pulsing, living heat of her. She was so very desirable. And he would prove to her that she had nothing to fear.

The dance was almost half over by the time Isobel mastered her panic. She needed to plan. She had to speak to him, to explain who she really was, but she did not dare to do so in the middle of this dance. What if there were a confrontation between them? Here, in public? That would spell ruin. She must wait.

But when the dance ended, he would escort her back to her chaperon. And then there would be proper introductions and—

Isobel took a deep breath and felt her pulse slow. She had to find another way of being alone with him. She crossed the set at that moment, just laying her hand on his as they turned together. Even through their evening gloves, she felt the warmth of his touch and the hidden strength of him. It crept along her arm and spread through her unresisting body.

In that instant, she understood, deep in her innermost being, that he was no monster. He was an Anstruther, but he was a fine, honourable man. She had let her stupid prejudices win, even when her whole being had known they were bound together by that first, magical encounter. She had told herself she was no Juliet with her forbidden Romeo, tumbling into love on sight. She had told herself that, unlike Juliet, she would marry the man her family chose, that she would do her duty.

But now he was here, touching her, and now she was become Juliet all over again, forgetting family, and feud, and duty.

She dared to smile up into his face. Hoping. But his answering smile was polite and fleeting.

She could not reach him here. She must find another way.

The dance ended. The ladies curtsied and the gentlemen bowed.

"Miss Lang, I—"

"Major Anstruther, I—" They broke off at the same moment. Isobel swallowed nervously. He was waiting courteously for her to speak first. "Thank you for the dance, Major. But it is exceedingly hot in here, do you not agree? Perhaps there is somewhere cooler, where I might take the air?"

The glance he gave her was eloquent. He was too well mannered to comment on such an obvious – and improper – ploy. Instead he ushered her across the ballroom and through tall curtained windows that led to a deserted terrace and a rather overgrown garden. He turned to leave.

"Major?"

He turned back. "I assumed you would wish me to fetch your chaperon, Miss Lang. You would not wish to be discovered out here alone with a man." His voice sounded strained, as if he were preventing his emotions from bubbling through by sheer force of will.

Was he remembering, perhaps? As she was? He was avoiding her eyes now, concentrating instead on ripping off his gloves.

"Major, I would wish..." Without thinking beyond her ungovernable desire for one last touch, she held out her hand to him. "I pray you will allow me to explain."

"There is no call for any explanation. You are a lady. You are not accountable to me. Not for anything you do." His voice was barely under control. His eyes were blazing with passion. He *was* remembering. But he was keeping his distance. He bowed stiffly. "If you will excuse me—"

"No!" She crossed the space between them in two quick steps and seized his arm with both hands. "There are things I must say to you. Please?"

She thought she felt a tiny tremor in the muscles of his forearm. He glanced over his shoulder at the curtained window and then down into the garden. "You must not be found alone with me here on the terrace. If you are determined on this...?" At Isobel's decisive

30

nod, he shrugged and laid his free hand briefly on hers. "As you wish. Let us go down into the garden. We must not be seen."

Before she could say a word more, he hurried her along the terrace and down the stone steps to the garden below. "It would be best if we avoided the gravel path, Miss Lang. Too much noise. There is no dew on the grass, so your evening slippers will not be spoiled."

She laughed nervously. She could not help it. "You have done this sort of thing before, I collect, sir?"

There was precious little light down here. She could barely see his face, but she thought she saw a brief smile twist the corner of his mouth.

"I have learned the importance of moving silently. But it has generally been in order to avoid the enemy." He was no longer so distant. He sounded almost like the man who had once kissed her into ecstasy.

This was the man she could deal with. "Only *generally*, sir?" Her tone was flirtatious. She was behaving like a wanton all over again. And she did not care.

For a fleeting moment, she allowed her fingers to press the flesh of his arm. This time, she was not mistaken about the tremor that ran through him.

"Miss Lang." The strain was back in his voice.

The warning was clear. She was testing his self-control. Good. "Have I said something wrong, sir?" Her tone was innocent. The way she clung to his arm was not. She wanted him

31

to feel the warmth of her body, to sense her urgency. More than anything, she wanted him to kiss her again. To rekindle those wonderful feelings.

Just once more.

Robert was conscious only of the twilight and the wide-eyed way she was gazing up at him under a sliver of moon and a canopy of stars. They were beautiful, but not as beautiful or as bright as Isobel's eyes.

He led her into the shadow of some tall bushes. "Well, Miss Lang?" His tone was rather stern, but it was the only way he could control his desire for her. She was too innocent to understand just how tempting she was. "You wished to…er…speak to me?"

She took a deep breath. Even in the gloom, he could see her white bosom swelling above the neckline of her gown. His body began to heat yet more.

"I have deceived you, Major. I am not who you think I am. For that, I apologise." She paused, avoiding his gaze. "But I am not sorry. For if I had told you the truth when we met again, you would have turned from me."

What on earth was she talking about? "I accept your apologies, of course, ma'am. But I am no wiser than before."

She swallowed. Her eyes grew even wider as she stared up at him. "You will think me very odd, sir. I had been taught from the cradle that all Anstruthers were wicked ogres. Yet you seemed to be a perfectly ordinary gentleman. That is— I mean, when we met that second time, you—"

"I restrained my inner ogre?"

That surprised another nervous laugh from her.

He put a hand over hers. "Did you fear it?" He was very serious now. He needed her to recognise that. That special enchantment was seeping into his veins, stoking his desire for her all over again.

"You know I did not." Her voice was a barely audible whisper. And her hands were shaking. She felt it, too. She was his nymph again.

It was too much. "Oh, God! Isobel!" Robert hauled her into his arms and began to kiss her. That first kiss – a lifetime ago – had been unlike anything he had ever known. He needed that magic again.

The moment his lips touched hers, there was a moan of pleasure in her throat and she began to respond eagerly, sliding her arms around his body and pressing her breasts against him. Within moments, they were kissing with deep and mutual passion. And Robert was stroking his fingers across the top of her breasts, where they strained to be free of her stays. Her fingers on his back were scrabbling up under his coat, desperately trying to reach his flesh.

They were on fire. Both of them.

He must not do this. They would be in full view of anyone who might wander out into the garden. She was being driven by desire. But she was also a lady, and an innocent, and much too young to know what she was risking in the throes of her first experience of passion.

She was too far gone to stop herself. Only Robert could save her.

He did not want to think about that. He continued to explore her luscious mouth and to stroke her body. She groaned again and pulled him even closer, their lips still exploring. Tormented beyond endurance, he picked her up in his arms and carried her as far as possible from the terrace and unwelcome intruders.

In the corner of the garden, hidden by trees and shrubs, he came upon a stone seat. As if it had been placed there to welcome them.

He sat down and settled her on his lap. That incredible kiss still continued, unbroken. He wanted her, so very much. She was, without doubt, the most desirable woman he had ever held in his arms.

The bodice of her gown was too tight to be pushed aside without damaging the fabric. He could only cup her breasts through the fine silk, but he could feel her nipples rising against his palms. Her desire, her passion was very real. If he could not touch her naked flesh there...

He laid his palm against her inner ankle. Skin on skin, separated only by the flimsiest silk stocking.

She gasped against his mouth. Then she clung to him. Slowly, slowly, he caressed his way up the inside of her leg until he reached her stocking top and her ribbon garter. He fingered it. Smooth, shiny, delightful. He allowed one finger to stray above to touch naked skin. Much more delightful. She was not resisting his advances. There was a tautness in her muscles, but he knew it was anticipation. She would follow his lead, just as she had done that first time. The way above was open to his questing hand. He stroked higher.

She gasped his name into his mouth. "Robert. Oh, Robert."

"My sweet Isobel." With a single long caress, he stroked up into the core of her. She was wide, and wet, and wanting. He could take her now, and she would welcome their joining. His body was aching for her, urging him on. They were both more than ready. Why not?

Because she was an innocent.

He stroked a finger across her moist heat, once, twice. She shivered. Once, and again. She was almost there.

He pushed a finger deep inside her, withdrew, pushed again. And stayed. He touched the ball of his thumb to the tiny nub. Once. His kiss was still deep, his tongue probing where the rest of his body could not.

He stroked her again. And again. Her scream of ecstasy was swallowed in his kiss. The spasms gripped her, held her taut, and then she collapsed against him with a gasp and a long groan.

It was over for her. And it must be over for him, too.

He had given her fulfilment, without risk of ruin. Anything more would dishonour them both.

He stroked her skirts and petticoats back to their proper place and sighed deeply. She was nestled in his arms like a trusting kitten. And he must not abuse that trust. "Isobel?"

"Mmm?" It was more a purr than anything else.

"You must go back to the house. If you should be found here with me—"

Her sharp intake of breath proved that reality had overtaken her at last. She must be blushing scarlet, but it was impossible to tell in the gloom.

"Take a little time to compose yourself, ma'am. Walk around the garden in the cool air for a few moments before you return to the ballroom. It will calm you." He put his hands to her waist and set her on her feet. Then he stood, too. "I will remain here where I cannot be seen. No one will know that we have been together. Go now." He gave her a little push.

"That is *all* you have to say? Is that all there *is*, Major Anstruther?" His trusting kitten was spitting angrily. "I have disgraced myself, I know. But you—"

He caught her back to him and held her close. "That is *not* all there is, Isobel. Unless you *do* think me an ogre?"

She shook her head. Her curls caressed his chin in the most seductive way.

He forced himself to ignore it and to laugh softly. "I am glad of it. But now you must go in."

"Yes, I see that. I…Robert, I have to tell you that—"

He silenced her with a long, gentle kiss on the lips and stepped back, ruthlessly suppressing the urge to go further. "Will you save me the supper dance? I would deem it an honour." His voice was unrecognisable in his own ears.

She opened her mouth to speak, but no words came out. She nodded. And then she fled, her yellow gown ghostly pale in the dim light.

CHAPTER FOUR

Isobel gazed around the noisy dining room. She had known it was a risk to have the supper dance with Robert Anstruther, for someone might mention his name to her Aunt Carmichael. But the old lady seemed more interested in playing cards than in acting as chaperon. After that first dance, she had hardly been in the ballroom at all.

Isobel embraced her good fortune, determined to ignore the seed of doubt that was trying to take root in her mind. She would find the right moment to tell Robert the truth. Later. Surely he was too honourable to blame her for a stupid feud? Especially after everything they had shared.

She had danced with him, and she had spent those precious minutes in the garden with him, when he had… Mmm. Yes. It had been even more wonderful than that first kiss, in the magic mist of Caerlaverock. She would remember everything that had happened between them, but later, slowly, when she was alone.

Robert was making his way back from the supper table, carrying two laden plates. He did not need to catch her eye. She could not help gazing at him. How fine he looked in his dress uniform – tall, strong, resolute, and yet so caring underneath. He was—

"I was not quite sure what you might like, and so I brought you a little of everything." He grinned as he took his place opposite her at the little table and beckoned a waiter to fill their glasses. "Do you—?"

"Isobel!" Lady Carmichael had materialised like the wicked fairy. Isobel could have sworn she was nowhere near the supper room and yet, here she was, looking like a dark thundercloud about to drench everyone with freezing rain. "We must leave."

"But Aunt, I—"

Robert rose and bowed to the new arrival. "Forgive me, ma'am. I should introduce myself. I—"

Lady Carmichael raised her chin and sniffed loudly. "The Ritchie family does not consort with Anstruthers. Isobel, we must leave at once. Come, let us fetch your cloak." She stretched out her arm imperiously. It summoned Isobel, and at the same time it barred Robert from approaching her. He might have been invisible.

Isobel threw one last beseeching glance at Robert's frozen fury and followed her aunt from the room.

Ritchie! She was Archibald Ritchie's daughter, that old devil's only child. She had surely been making a may-game of Robert from the moment he told her his name. She was no better than the rest of the infernal Ritchie clan.

He looked up to see his hostess approaching his table, with one of her gawky daughters beside her. That was more than he could stomach.

He rose and bowed. "Mrs Rougely, I must beg your indulgence. I have to leave. If you will excuse me." Without giving her a chance to reply, he hurried towards the door. He must get away from this place before it suffocated him.

Outside, in the cooler air, he began to walk vaguely in the direction of his rooms, trying to make sense of the seething mass of ideas and emotions that was threatening to make his head explode.

She was little better than a strumpet. No wonder, since she was a Ritchie.

He put a hand to the hilt of his dress sword. Just at this moment, he wanted to draw it and run someone through. Preferably Isobel Ritchie.

He groaned aloud. No, that wasn't true.

That wasn't what he wanted at all. He would never be able to hurt a hair of her head. She had ensnared him at that very first meeting when she had returned his kiss with such innocent sweetness. That had been *his* doing, not hers. She was no strumpet.

But what about tonight, in the garden? She had willingly gone with him. Alone. Had she been trying to seduce him? She would not be the first to try to compromise him into making an offer of marriage.

She was just like the rest of them. She must be.

No. She was not.

He had almost seduced her, but she had not demanded marriage. She had not demanded anything. She had wanted to explain.

He groaned aloud. He had been an utter fool. She had been trying to tell him who she was, but he had been so driven by desire that he had not let her speak. He had been overcome by his need to take her in his arms again, to kiss her till they were both mindless with passion.

Which was what he had done. And more.

Isobel Ritchie, enemy and siren, was too beautiful, too spirited, too passionate about life to be condemned without a hearing because of an ancient feud between their families. He wanted her more than he had ever wanted any woman. Ritchie or no, she was like a drug coursing through his veins. He would never be rid of it – of the magic she had woven around him – until he saw her again and discovered the whole truth of what she was.

* * *

Alone in the safety of her own room, Isobel was sorely tempted to throw things. Preferably things that would shatter into tiny pieces.

Sir Hugh and Lady Carmichael had called her a disgrace to the Ritchie name. They had threatened to send her back to Scotland, though they all knew it was an empty threat. The family could not afford to waste Isobel's one chance of snaring a wealthy husband.

Robert was wealthy. He was the sole heir to huge estates. He held the King's commission. As a potential suitor, he would be eligible in every way. Except for being an Anstruther.

But Isobel's father would never consent to her marriage to the age-old enemy of her family, even if Robert could bring himself to propose. Why would he? He was furious at her deception. He must hate her now for who she was and what she had done.

She could have told him the truth. She had failed, and now she had lost him. By her own stupidity, she had lost the man she loved.

Love?

It should have come as a shock to realise that she loved Robert Anstruther. It did not. It was like the recognition of an old friend, a welcome reunion with a truth she had always known. He had appeared to her like a ghost from the past, emerging from the gloom of those crumbling ruins. He had walked out of the twilight and into her heart.

But her idyll had shattered with one word. *Ritchie.* She would never see him again.

* * *

Robert paced the gravel path of the Chelsea Physic Garden. Would she come?

It had taken him two frustrating days to contrive this meeting through the old nurse. He had spent the whole time thinking of nothing but Isobel Ritchie, nymph and nemesis. Had she laid a spell on him, like a witch?

He shook his head at his own stupidity. She was an innocent. If he was bewitched, it was his own doing.

And still he did not know if she would come.

He glanced up at the huge cedars. They were certainly magnificent. Unfortunately, they were also famous, drawing many visitors to this exotic garden. Some of them were even beginning to throw enquiring glances at the uniformed officer who was pacing up and down the path.

Robert slowed and forced himself to breathe deeply. He had every reason to be furious at Isobel's deception, but he must, in honour, give her a chance to explain. Even a Ritchie might have preserved some shred of honour. And after what they had done together—

He would not allow himself to remember that. It was enough that he had so nearly ravished her. He had no right to question her Ritchie honour when he had betrayed his own. If she did come, it was he who should apologise. If she—

"Why, Major Anstruther. What a surprise!"

Shocked, Robert spun round. She was here. And she looked beautiful enough to rival any flower in this garden. She was wearing a sprigged muslin gown, with a vibrant leaf-green and gold shawl draped across her arms. A straw hat was perched at a jaunty angle on top of her red-gold curls and tied under her ear with a huge bow of green ribbon. She looked good enough to kiss.

Or to devour.

But her smile was uncertain and very distant.

Robert bowed. He smiled back but made no move towards her. If only he had not chosen such a public place. "How delightful to meet you again, Miss Ritchie. May I say that you are wearing a very fetching hat?"

He let his gaze rest on her face.

Her smile widened a fraction. Now, it was echoed in her eyes.

"If you wish to walk around the gardens, may I offer you my escort, ma'am? I am at your service."

She nodded, with a fluttering of green ribbons. Then she turned to her maid. "You may walk behind, Annie." Without waiting for a response, she slid her arm through Robert's and they began to stroll along the path.

How very proper. A young lady walking with a gentleman in a public place, with her maid a few yards behind. Close enough to watch, but not close enough to hear.

"Miss Ritchie. Isobel, I think there are matters we must discuss. About our previous meetings. You—"

She stopped him with a slight pressure of her gloved fingers on his arm. "Major Anstruther, I have come to beg your pardon. For everything. And to ask for your continued discretion. You see, I—" Her voice cracked.

She swallowed, and began again. "Major Anstruther, I must tell you that a marriage is being arranged for me. By my uncle."

He had been trying to nurse his righteous fury for days. Now it was gone in an instant, like air from a punctured balloon. His whole body turned icy cold. He was going to lose her. And all to fill the Ritchie coffers, to replace the fortune her father had wasted in pursuit of an ancient feud. Lives would be ruined for the sake of Archibald Ritchie's stubborn pride.

Robert realised, shocked, that his own father was little better. He could have ended the feud, but he had not.

It was a full minute before Robert could control the bitterness and frustration that flooded through him, and allow himself to speak. "Have you agreed to it?" he snapped.

She gasped. The colour drained from her face.

"The gentleman is wealthy, of course. May I know his name?"

She drew herself up haughtily, though she did not remove her hand from his arm. "You go too far, Major. You do not own me."

She was alone, facing a loveless marriage for the sake of her family. What was Robert's plight compared with Isobel's? Her burden would last a lifetime.

He dared to touch his hand to hers. "Forgive

46

me. I had no right to speak so. Miss Ritchie, I must be honest with you, even if my words should give you pain. I asked you to meet me here today, because I intended to ring a peal over you for your deception."

She shivered and turned ashen. Her fingers gripped convulsively on his arm. Her free hand went to her mouth, as if she were about to retch.

His stomach clenched painfully at the sight of the distress he had caused. Words rushed out, unbidden. "And to make you a proposal of marriage."

He had said it.

He had not meant to. But, as soon as the words were spoken, he knew she was exactly what he wanted, what he needed. He did not care a straw who her family was. Their idiotic feud could go hang.

She was silent for a long time. "*Intended*, sir?" she whispered at last. "I take it that you have now changed your mind?"

He bit back a curse. "No, I have not! I would go down on one knee, here on this path, if I thought it would win you."

"I pray you will do no such thing, sir," she said instantly. "Think of the scandal."

"It is only because I *am* thinking of the scandal, and of the need to protect your reputation, that I do not take you in my arms and carry you off this minute. Isobel, will you not have me? I know we can find a way to—"

"Your agitation is starting to attract attention, sir. Let us continue to stroll."

She was right. She was proving a much

better tactician than he was. What on earth was happening to him?

They continued for several minutes. Isobel spoke knowledgeably about various plants. The matter-of-fact discussion seemed to calm them both.

He dropped his voice. "I ask your pardon for my outburst, ma'am. But I must ask you to believe that I am sincere in my proposal of marriage."

She nodded slightly. She was looking straight ahead as they walked, but he knew she was listening intently.

"I do understand your dilemma. Marriage to me would cause a rift between you and your family. Marriage to the man they have chosen would save your father from ruin." When she did not reply, he ventured, "Will you tell me about him? Your suitor?"

She sighed. "It is almost the end of the season. No gentleman has offered for me."

"But I—"

"No *suitable* gentleman has offered for me. My family cannot afford another season. All that money—" she touched her muslin skirts and let them drop again "—has achieved nothing. And so my uncle has found another solution."

She swallowed hard. "His name is James Craigie. You would not be acquainted with him for he is a...a well-to-do merchant from Edinburgh. He has four pretty young daughters and he...he wants them to marry into society. He is prepared to pay to secure a second wife who can smooth their path." She shook her head. "He must truly love his girls, for my uncle has priced me very high indeed."

Robert bit back a curse. "Isobel," he said in a low voice, "the Anstruther estates are some of the richest in Scotland. I will pay double what your uncle asks. Forget this confounded feud. Marry me!"

"My father would prefer ruin to such a union. And I am sure your own father would be just as much opposed. It is my duty to go through with this marriage. And it is your duty to forget me. We must not meet again. I am sorry, Robert." She lingered over his name. He fancied her eyes were sheened with tears but she turned her head away before he could be sure. He was losing her.

They had reached one of the great trees. He pulled her round behind it and pressed her back against the trunk. Then he kissed her, hard and long and demanding. She tried to resist, but that lasted only seconds. Then she was kissing him back, pulling him closer, touching his cheek.

"Miss Isobel!"

They broke apart at the sound of the maid's outraged voice.

"Begone, woman," Robert snarled.

The maid recoiled.

"Isobel, there is more to marriage than money. Or duty. You know that. Have we not just proved it?" He touched a fingertip to her lower lip.

She said nothing. She straightened so that her back was no longer against the tree trunk. Then she stared at the ground.

"Isobel, beautiful Isobel, marry me. I will find a way to make it right with your family. I swear I will."

She looked up. Her eyes were wide and glistening. "What about your own family? What if your father should disown you? What then?"

He had not thought of that. He had not thought of anything except that sudden, all-encompassing fear that he would lose her. It was true he was the only child, but the Anstruther estate was not entailed. He had promised her the wealth of his family estates, but he did not yet own them. What if he never did?

He had his army pay. And he had a modest inheritance from his mother. It was not much, but it would allow them to live on the fringes of society. They might even live better than the Ritchies did now. Surely that was preferable to marriage to the merchant Craigie?

"I am not dependent on my father, Isobel. In any case, I do not believe he would cast me off, especially not once he has met you." Was that the truth? Robert could not be sure. His conscience prompted him to add, "Even if he did disown me, I could provide for you. We would manage well enough."

She had not moved. He seized her hand and pressed a kiss into her palm. "Isobel, dear Isobel, I want you for my wife. I *need* you for my wife. Will you have me?"

She bent her head, her voice the merest whisper. "Forsaking all others."

The words of the marriage service. Did that

mean she agreed? "Isobel?"

Instead of replying, she tucked her arm under his and drew him back to the path. She began to walk slowly towards the exit.

"Robert, you ask me to choose between you and my family, between lo—" She stopped. She had flushed a pale rose pink. "You ask me to choose between my inclination and my duty. I cannot decide now, here with you. Will you give me time to think?"

"If you will at least consider my offer."

"I will. I promise I will. But I must return home before I am missed."

"How will I know your answer? When will I see you again?"

"I will send Annie to you."

"You will not use her to—?"

She shook her head at him. "Whatever my answer, Robert, I promise I will deliver it to you in person. And now we must part." She withdrew her arm and dropped a polite curtsy. "Thank you so much for your escort, Major Anstruther," she said brightly. "It has been a pleasure. I hope we may meet again before the end of the season. Good day to you, sir."

With that, she beckoned to her maid and started for the exit at a brisk pace. She did not look back.

"Miss Isobel?" Annie had kept silent since they entered the carriage at the Physic Garden, but now she reached out a hand to clasp Isobel's. "For 'tis hard, my lamb, choosing between yer family and the man ye love."

"What? Annie, what makes you think—?"

"I don't *think*, lassie, I know. And I'll stay at yer side, whatever ye do."

Isobel fumbled for her handkerchief and blew her nose. She would *not* cry. She had a choice to make, and precious little time to think about it.

What could she do? She would not be permitted to refuse Mr Craigie's offer once it was made. There was no salvation by that route.

Robert had sworn he would find a way to make it right. Did she dare to believe him? Did she trust him enough to abandon her family, and her duty, simply for love? He wanted her. He had even admitted he needed her. But he had not said he loved her.

Oh, it was tearing her apart. Love? Or duty? If she married Robert, if he did not succeed in reconciling their families, Isobel's father would be left almost destitute. Could she bear to have that on her conscience?

It was so easy for Juliet and her Romeo. Juliet did not have a family on the point of ruin. And she had Friar Lawrence to help her to follow her heart.

The lovers had to die to end the feud.

Oh, ridiculous. It would never come to that. There must be a way of persuading Isobel's father to accept Robert. Surely she could find a way?

The germ of a mad, impossible, outrageous idea settled in Isobel's mind and began to grow.

CHAPTER FIVE

ROBERT STOOD STARING DOWN INTO THE fire, her hasty note loose in his fingers. It was madness. Utter madness. How could an innocent girl even think of such a thing? For she *was* innocent. He would take his oath on it. She—

"Shall I light the candles, Major?" It was Grant, Robert's army batman, quietly efficient as ever.

Robert folded the paper and stowed it in his pocket. "I am expecting a young lady visitor, Grant. She must come and go without being seen."

Grant began to light the candles on the side tables. "That can be arranged, sir." He had not shown even a flicker of surprise. He finished stacking the piles of maps on the desk and looked up enquiringly. "You will not be wanting to discuss battle tactics tonight, I assume, sir? Shall I put these back in the store room?"

Battle tactics? With Isobel? Robert was shocked into a bark of laughter. "Yes, if you must." He watched as Grant collected up the maps and other military papers and crossed to the furthest bookcase. When he touched the hidden spring, the bookcase opened a little way, like a door. Behind it lay the windowless room that the original owner had used as a private gambling hell. It was as dark and forbidding as a prison.

Grant closed the bookcase again. "Shall I light the candles in the bedchamber as well, Major?"

"No. What the devil should I want with candles there at this hour?"

His traitorous body knew the answer all too well.

"Miss Smith has arrived, sir."

Robert had heard no knock, nor the opening of the street door, yet suddenly she was here, standing in his hallway. She was closely wrapped in a thick dark cloak, with a heavily-veiled bonnet obscuring her face.

He would have known her anywhere.

"You are welcome, Miss...er...Smith. That will be all, Grant."

The moment the door closed, Robert

propelled her into his sitting room and demanded angrily, "Have you the least idea of how dangerous this is? Visiting a man, unchaperoned, at this time of night? What if you should be recognised?"

"Your man saw to it that I was not. And I am safer here than anywhere else we might meet, as I told you in my note. I believe my uncle is suspicious. He has employed a strange new manservant, who follows me when I go out."

"And has he followed you here?"

She put back her veil. "No. I made sure my departure was not observed."

He could well believe it. Isobel Ritchie was no man's fool. "Have you decided? Do you have a response to my offer?" The words burst from him. His voice sounded much too sharp, even in his own ears. What was it about this girl that made him lose every last vestige of control?

She appeared quite unconcerned. She strolled across to the roaring fire, stripped off her gloves and held out her hands to warm. Then, quite casually, she untied her bonnet and flung it on to a chair. Her cloak followed. Underneath, she was wearing a ravishing evening gown of deep red silk, in an extremely low-cut style that would not have disgraced a member of the muslin company. Her choice of dress was outrageous.

And yet the sight of her stirred his blood.

She looked across at him and smiled. Too knowingly. She must be perfectly well aware of his physical reaction to her beauty. No doubt she had dressed for just such an effect.

55

A warning voice thrummed in his brain. In that moment of madness in Chelsea, he had offered for Isobel Ritchie, believing her innocent, and cruelly used by her appalling family. But now she was behaving like a practised courtesan. Had she lured him into proposing by firing his lust at the prospect of a rival? Did Craigie even exist?

She was a Ritchie, bred in the bone. It would be sweet revenge to take Robert's wealth and then cuckold him, the moment she had his ring upon her finger.

He hated to believe such a thing of his twilight nymph. He knew he was letting ancient prejudice drive him. And yet he had to admit that it all fitted much too well.

Especially with a Ritchie.

Doubt was eating at him. He frowned sternly at her. "That gown, if you will permit me to say so, ma'am, is rather too daring for an unmarried lady. It provokes quite the wrong response in any red-blooded male. May I fetch you a wrap?"

"You have a supply of ladies' wraps here? How…er…unusual."

She was baiting him, probably quite deliberately. It was too artful by half. But however practised she was, she would not be allowed to win. "I am sure I can find something that will serve, Miss Ritchie. A towel, a quilt, a bed sheet, perhaps?"

"A bed sheet?" A slow, sensuous smile touched her mouth. "Yes, pray do fetch me one of those."

"I ought to strangle you with it," he

muttered darkly, pushing past her to open the bedchamber door.

She caught his arm before he could do so. "Robert."

He stopped dead. The touch of her fingers had set his arm aglow, and then the rest of his body. It was sheer torture. And she must know it.

"Robert, I have come here to...to offer to share your bed. If you want me."

By the time her incredible words were out, she was blushing to the depths of her décolletage.

The change floored him. How could he doubt her? She must be a true innocent. Only an innocent could blush like that. Surely it must be so?

She was staring at the floor, twisting her fingers together. Her earlier assurance had totally vanished. It must have been an act.

But why?

He seized her by the shoulders. He wanted to shake the truth out of her, but he knew he could never do such a thing to her, no matter what she was. She was here alone, completely in his power, and she would leave here as untouched as she had come.

No, not untouched.

She herself did not wish for that. She was offering to share his bed. And without having given him an answer to his proposal.

He understood it all then. Of course! She was going to turn him down. However much she valued Robert, she valued duty, and family, more. But she was too honest to pretend that there was nothing between them. So she had come to give him a farewell gift, the gift of herself. And to ensure that he could not refuse her, she had chosen to play the coquette, to feed his lust until it overcame all sense of honour.

Fear and anger gripped him, in equal measure. He could not prevent it from showing in his voice when he spoke. "I will not let you do this. You would dishonour us both. I will not send you – deflowered – to marry another man."

She did not try to struggle free of his grasp. Nor did she look up at him. Her words, when they came, were barely audible. "If I am to defy my family, Robert, I...I must be sure of you. That is why I offered—" She hid her burning face in her hands.

His heart began to gallop. Had he been so very wrong? "You *will* marry me, Isobel? Truly?"

"Yes," she whispered. She raised her head. Her eyes were dry, but anguished. "Because you promised you would make it right for my family. You have offered me a way of reconciling my duty with my...with my desire. Robert, I am trusting you to fulfil your promise!"

"On my honour, I shall find a way to do so."

It was a solemn vow. Somehow, he would do it. For this Ritchie siren who fired his blood to the point of madness.

He dropped his hands from her tender flesh and took a step back. He had surely been mistaken in thinking her practised in the art of seduction. He must not treat her as if she were.

He cast a quick glance towards the open door and the bed beyond. "Isobel, I— Isobel, there is no need for this. I do desire you – you know I do – but it can wait until after we are married."

"No." She moved to slide her hands behind his neck and draw him close. "No. This is what I want. Now. To seal our bargain. Kiss me, Robert."

For a moment, he tried to resist. But the touch of her lips on his was magic, conjuring up all the enchantment of that first twilight encounter.

It began again as a simple kiss. Then, as desire mounted, it became a kiss of commitment, and of longing, with an exciting edge, for longing was about to become fulfilment. They both knew that now.

Isobel dared to relax into him at last. Her spiky, top-lofty behaviour had been an act, a cloak to cover her fear of rejection. He had said he wanted her, and even that he needed her. But she was demanding that he mend a feud that had lasted for centuries. That was a huge price to ask from a man who did not love her. No sensible man would ever pay it, no matter how strong his body's urges.

As the kiss deepened, Isobel understood that Robert was not that sensible man. Her hopes emerged like a budding flower. She would give herself to him, now, and then her love would be able to bloom in the sanctity of marriage.

When they parted, both were gasping for breath.

Isobel looked him full in the face. What she saw in his eyes drained the last of the tension from her body. She let it go in a long sigh. He did want her. She could not tell exactly what he felt for her, but it was much more than mere lust.

"You sigh? What is the matter, sweet?" He sounded unsure. A bold soldier, veteran of many campaigns, *unsure* in the face of a willing virgin?

That wicked thought curled her mouth into a knowing smile. "Absolutely nothing is the matter. I was afraid this moment might never come. And now that it has..."

This was no time for words. She pulled his mouth back down to hers and kissed him eagerly. His groaning response shivered all the way down to her toes.

Robert deepened the kiss. The warmth of his embrace tingled against the bare skin of her arms and throat. It was as if she were so near the fire that her skin was starting to scorch. Yet this burning was wonderful. She wanted more and more, even if it should burn her up. This time, she would return his kiss in full measure. His tongue touched and withdrew. When he touched again, it was only just to the inside of her lips. He was tempting her to come to him. Did she dare?

She could not resist the taste of heaven that he offered. She touched her tongue between his lips, and beyond. He put a hand to the back of her head, pulling her mouth even closer. Encouraged, she went further and soon their tongues were twining and dancing together. It made her bones melt.

"Oh, Isobel," he groaned into her mouth. It was a deep, primitive sound, like nothing she had ever heard before, even in his arms. He broke the kiss. "Oh, Isobel," he said again. There was such strain in his face as he gazed down into her eyes. "Are you truly sure you want this?"

Ah. Even now, he was prepared to stop, for her sake. She would not permit it. She had no words. Instead, she lifted his hand to her lips and kissed his open palm. Then she led him into his own bedchamber. The bed looked huge, dominating the whole room, but she was not afraid. She raised his free hand to her lips for another kiss. She could not bring herself to speak. She had been brazen enough already.

He seemed to understand her need. He cupped both her hands in his and raised them to his lips, kissing first one palm and then the other, with such gentleness yet such desire that she shivered.

Was that what her kiss had done to him? She fervently hoped so.

He pulled her close and began to kiss her face, her neck, parading tiny kisses from her ear lobe all the way down to her breasts. They seemed to respond to the touch of his mouth, swelling as if trying to escape from the confines of her borrowed gown. It was almost indecent, but she had chosen it deliberately, to tempt him.

And it had. Yet the temptation was biting into her, too. "I want to take this off." Oh, goodness! Had she said that out loud?

His deep chuckle against her skin proved that she had. "Soon, my lady, soon." He flicked his tongue across the top of her breast, just where it sank behind the constricting wall of her bodice. His hand cupped her through the fabric. She strained towards him. If only...

And then her breast was free. Somehow, he had pushed the fabric aside so that he could roll one longing nipple back and forth between finger and thumb. It was torture. She groaned. Then even greater torture, for he took it in his mouth and sucked so strongly that she felt the pull all through her body. Desire grew and settled at the junction of her thighs with hot, heavy longing. She gasped out his name.

"That is a most beautiful gown, but you will be much more beautiful without it." He led her across to the fireplace, for there were no lights in the room. He bent to touch a spill to the hearth and lit two candles. "Mmm. Better. I want to see you."

With caressing hands, he turned her round and round, touching, admiring, dropping tiny kisses on exposed flesh. "Beautiful. And about to become more so." He undid the fastenings of her gown and pushed it to the floor. Her petticoats followed. And then he bent to kiss her breasts, above her stays.

She could feel his fingers at her back, deftly undoing her laces while, at the same time, he sucked eagerly on her breast. The combination was so arousing that her knees turned to water.

They buckled, just as he pushed her loosened stays from her body.

"Ah." He caught her into his arms. "You are a diamond." He lifted her and carried her across to the bed where he set her down for a second, threw back the coverlet, and laid her on the cool, smooth sheets. He removed her shoes and kissed her ribbon garters. He started to kiss her outer thigh, just above her stocking. Then he kissed his way across to the soft skin of her inner leg, the tiny beginnings of his stubble teasing through the silken mesh.

She let her thighs fall apart. This was what she wanted. This was the way to fulfilment.

He undid her garters and slowly rolled her stockings down to her feet, kissing all the way. It took his mouth away from the core of her, where she wanted him to be. It was tantalising, torturing. Wonderful.

She was floating away, eyes closed, as if on a supporting cloud. But suddenly he was gone. She opened her eyes. He was standing near the fireplace, with one of the candlesticks in his hand. And he was laughing.

"One day—" He was laughing so much he could barely speak the words. "One day, that rogue of mine will meet his match." He raised the candle so that its light fell on a small table in the darkest corner of the room. On it stood a bottle of champagne and two glasses. Robert threw her a rueful smile and reached for the bottle. "My batman, I fear, is too clever by half. But, on this occasion—" He paused, gazing across at Isobel. She knew she looked like a wanton, spread across his bed, clad only in a chemise that clung damply to her curves and concealed nothing at all. "You look good enough to eat." He began to twist open the champagne. "Or to drink," he added wickedly.

In a moment, he was carrying two full glasses to the bedside. He returned for the bottle, and the candle. "Champagne, my sweet?"

She nodded and moistened her lips with the tip of her tongue. His response was a sharp intake of breath, as she sat up and reached for her glass. She sipped, and swallowed, and sipped again. He simply watched her. Then he took the glass from her fingers and set it down. He had not touched his own.

"I find the touch of glass on my lips much too cold and hard." He put his hands to the hem of her chemise. Slowly, reverently, he pulled it up and over her head. At last, she was totally, blissfully, naked in the bed of the man she loved.

"Oh, yes," he breathed, and gently pushed her back on to the pillows.

Now he would remove his own clothing and join her, surely? But he did not. He was standing on the floor beside the bed. He bent to drop a kiss between her breasts and then on, down past her ribcage and over her flat stomach. "Not hard, not cold."

She relaxed into the pillows and closed her eyes. She would not try to predict what he would do. Fulfilment would come, and the journey would be wonderful.

"You are the most beautiful vessel any man could ever drink from."

What? She opened her eyes to see him holding a champagne glass just above her breasts. He was smiling wickedly down at her. Then he caught both her wrists in his free hand and held her arms above her head. Her eyes widened. He was going to—

He tilted the glass so that a single drop fell on to her burning skin. It should have fizzed into steam like water dropped on hot coals. She struggled a little against his hold, trying to free her hands. She had to touch him. "Robert! Please. I need to—" He laughed, low in his throat, and let her go. Then he began to drip yet more tiny bubbles on to her skin, until the tingling drops were running down towards her navel. When he bent to retrieve them with his mouth, she put her hands to his head and raked her fingers through his hair, pushing him even closer.

He licked the wine from her skin with a deep moan of satisfaction. And then he began all over again. Now he dipped the tip of his tongue into the tiny pool of golden liquid and licked his way up to her breast, circling her aching nipple tantalisingly. He did not touch the swollen, straining flesh that so yearned for the feel of his mouth. Then he paused to admire his handiwork before repeating the process with her other breast. "Champagne never tasted so wonderful before."

A few more drops. This time, he licked them from the valley between her breasts down to her navel. And beyond.

And then he was kissing her so strongly that her hips bucked off the bed to meet his

65

questing mouth. In moments, she was spiralling out of control. The spasms seized her and took her over the edge into blissful oblivion.

CHAPTER SIX

"ISOBEL? COME BACK TO ME?"

She opened her eyes to find that she was no longer alone in the great bed. Robert was beside her at last, and as naked as she. "Oh." He stroked a finger down her cheek, so very gently. "Mmm." Her body felt soft and languid. She turned into his arms, seeking his embrace.

This time, he did not resist. He accepted what she offered, kissing her deeply, holding her close against his aroused body, running his caressing hand down her back to cup her bottom and pull her closer still. He tasted of champagne, and lovemaking. The hard length of him pressed against her belly. She gloried in the feel of him, skin against skin, flesh against flesh.

Soon to be one flesh.

They kissed until they were both moaning. He rolled her on to her back and began to caress her breasts, her belly, her flanks, with long sweeping strokes, but never coming near the core of her. He caressed her until she was almost screaming with need.

"Touch me, Robert," she groaned into his hungry mouth. "I need you now. Please."

He put his hands to her face and held her steady while he settled into the welcoming cradle of her hips. "Look at me, Isobel. Trust me."

He held her gaze and drove into her moist heat with one long stroke. Joy, wonder and then a sharp pain. She screwed up her eyes. She could not help it. He caught her shocked gasp in a consoling kiss and held himself very still within her, waiting. Very tenderly, he kissed her closed eyelids until her muscles relaxed once more.

"Isobel?" His voice was very soft. And concerned.

For her.

She opened her eyes and gazed up at him. She could see the flame of that single candle reflected there. He was frowning. She lifted a finger to smooth his brow. She felt her body softening, stretching and moulding itself around him. That momentary pain was gone. His heat was within her, leashed by his iron will until she should be ready for him. The flames began to leap within her body. She wanted him. She wanted this.

Without knowing what she did, she tensed her inner muscles around him. His response was instant. He pushed even further into the core of her as she opened to him. Seconds later, she was wrapping her legs around him and straining to match the rhythm of his long strokes.

Harder, higher, faster. Together. They were moving as one flesh, and it was glorious. She could no longer think. She could only feel. And then he took her beyond feeling, beyond thought, into ecstasy.

Having Isobel in his arms, in his bed, was bliss. There could be no more doubt. She had been innocent. And untouched. Now she was his. Completely.

He dropped a kiss on her hair, but did nothing more. He did not want to wake her. Soon they would have to plan what to do, how to return her to her uncle's house without detection. None of it would be easy. For now, let her sleep.

A loud banging on the front door made him start up. It was long after midnight. Who on earth could that be, making such an infernal din?

"Oh, heavens. My uncle!" She was instantly wide awake.

"What? How do you know?" Had she planned this? Was it a trap?

"I...I don't. But who else could it be at this time of night? That man, my uncle's spy, he must have followed me after all." She put her hands to her flaming cheeks. Her eyes were wide and staring, proving she was just as shocked as he was.

She gave a strangled laugh. To Robert's ears, she sounded almost hysterical. "When my uncle finds me here, he will have no option but to agree to our marriage."

"More like to shoot us both," he said brutally.

She gasped in horror. Faced with stark reality, she was terrified.

He knew he had been wrong to doubt her. He tilted up her face so she was forced to look at him. He tried to smile reassuringly. "Isobel, you are a darling girl, but you would be the death of both of us. You must not be found here. Not like this."

"But I—"

He silenced her with a finger across her lips. No time for argument. She was his now. He must save her. "Do you trust me enough to do exactly as I say?"

She nodded, wide-eyed.

"Help me collect up your things. Quickly." He scooped up her discarded clothes and pushed them into her arms. Then he wrapped his silk dressing gown round her naked body. Grabbing the champagne bottle and glasses, he hurried her into his sitting room. He pressed the spring to open the hidden door and bundled her through, followed by the wine and her outdoor clothes. "Stay there. Don't move or make a sound until I come to release you. It may take me some time to convince your uncle." He dropped a quick hard kiss on her mouth and pushed her down to sit on his army trunk. "Sorry, sweetheart. Daren't risk a candle." With that, he closed the door on her, leaving her alone in the dark.

She had courage. She would not cry out.

He could hear Grant's loudly muttered complaints as he walked slowly to the door. The servant did not need to be told what to do. He would make a great fuss and delay Sir Hugh as long as possible.

Robert raced back into his bedchamber. He had no dressing gown now, of course. He ripped open the clothes press and quickly threw a fresh nightshirt over his head. Then he set about putting the bed to rights. In moments, it was done. It looked as though only one side had been used.

Robert's clothes still littered the floor. No time to retrieve them. Let it look as if an idle gentleman had simply dropped his clothing for his valet to pick up. Sir Hugh would not be surprised.

Robert stuck his feet into his slippers, picked up the lighted candle from the nightstand and marched out into the hallway. "What the hell is going on?" he thundered.

The door was open. An elderly gentleman stood on the threshold, flanked by a thick-set man with the face of a prizefighter.

"Grant, inform this *gentleman* that I am not at home to visitors."

The batman had barely opened his mouth to obey when the visitor pushed him aside and stepped into the hallway. He was almost purple with rage.

"I am Sir Hugh Carmichael. Isobel Ritchie is my niece. I know you have her here, Anstruther. To debauch her, no doubt. Exactly the kind of behaviour I would expect from one of your ilk. I demand that you produce her. At once!"

"You are mistaken, sir," Robert answered quietly. He had not moved. He stood blocking Sir Hugh's path to the inner rooms.

"You defy me, sir?" Sir Hugh produced a small pistol and pointed it at Robert's heart. "Stand aside. I will look for myself."

Robert sighed theatrically. "If that is Sir Hugh's man standing on the step, Grant, pray bring him into the hall. And close the door. I prefer not to have my business trumpeted to all the street. Especially when an innocent lady's reputation is at stake."

Sir Hugh was shaking with fury. His pistol was far from steady.

Robert faced him squarely. "Your accusation is extremely serious, sir. It goes to my honour as well as that of your niece. Perhaps you would now withdraw it?"

"Isobel is gone from my house," Sir Hugh barked. "My man informs me that she is with you."

"Ah. Now I understand your agitation. However, you are wrong."

Sir Hugh did not move or speak.

"Sir, I must ask you to take care what you do," Robert continued blandly. "Shooting an unarmed man is murder, you know. Even an Anstruther."

The pistol was lowered a little. The shaking had stopped. Sir Hugh seemed to be recovering his self-control. "Major Anstruther, will you look me in the eye and swear, on your honour as an officer and a gentleman, that Isobel Ritchie is not here in your house?"

Robert replied without even a blink. "I will do better than that, Sir Hugh." He stood aside and gestured towards the open door. "In deference to your years, and to your understandable concern for the reputation of your niece, I will permit you to search my rooms. Pray, go through. Search wherever you wish. There are not many potential hiding places, but I do recommend you look under the bed."

Sir Hugh seemed taken aback for a second, but then he pocketed his pistol and marched into Robert's sitting room. Bookcases, tables and chairs, a sofa and a desk. There was no possible hiding place. He pulled back the long heavy curtains. The window recess was empty.

Robert followed him into the bedchamber and threw open all the doors to cupboards and presses. Nothing. He threw back the window curtains. Again nothing. He watched with some satisfaction as the older man knelt to look under the bed. Nothing. Of course.

Sir Hugh stood up a little shakily. He eyed the bed in silence, assessing the bumps and hollows. It did not look like a scene of passionate love-making. Robert was confident of that.

"Anstruther, I—"

"You will wish to check the other rooms,

too. Grant!" His batman appeared instantly. "Sir Hugh has seen this room and my sitting room. Take him through to the other rooms and make sure he sees everything. I would have no suspicion remaining that I am concealing Miss Ritchie."

With drooping shoulders, Sir Hugh followed the batman out. Robert grabbed his discarded shirt and breeches from the floor and dressed with the speed of a soldier summoned to face the enemy.

By the time Sir Hugh returned to the sitting room, his high colour was gone. His skin was grey. "It seems I was wrong. She is not here." He was avoiding Robert's eye.

"Sir, I am glad you are now satisfied. Believe me, I do understand your concern. Your niece is young and vulnerable. She should not be out alone in London. Perhaps she has gone to stay with a female friend?"

"Yes, it is possible, I suppose. I can only hope you are right, Major. I...I ask you to excuse me for having forced my way in here. I had information that—"

Robert stopped him with a wave of his hand. If Sir Hugh made Robert a grovelling apology, it would lead to even more bad blood once the truth was known. "Let us forget this ever happened, sir. I am sure you will be wishing to return home quickly, in case there is more reliable news of where Miss Ritchie may have gone. I pray there will be."

He ushered Sir Hugh into the hallway and then out of the house. The bruiser, who had neither moved nor spoken, followed his master out.

Robert closed the door with slightly shaky hands and leant against it, letting out a long breath. His Isobel. He had saved her.

But for how long?

"Grant, go and organise a chaise and four. I shall need it here in two hours. We leave as soon as it is light."

"Aye, sir. Which road shall you be taking?"

"The road north. As I am sure you already knew." He grinned suddenly. "We have a battle to win, Grant, and our forces are few. So we shall need to use guile, not a frontal attack. Say as little as possible at the posting house, and return quickly. I shall need you to remain here in London, as rearguard."

"Aye, sir. You may rely on me to deal with Sir Hugh, and his bruiser."

The moment the batman left, Robert rushed across to the secret door. Poor Isobel had been locked inside for what must have seemed like hours. In the dark, with no way of knowing when she would be freed.

Robert touched the spring. As the door swung open, he lifted a branch of candles from the side table and held it high. "Isobel?"

She was blinking blindly against the light. She had pushed her arms into the sleeves of his dressing gown and tied the belt at her waist, but otherwise she had not moved. Her clothes lay in a pile on the floor. Her hands were clasped together in her lap. Robert fancied it was to stop them from shaking.

He put his free arm round her shoulders. Poor girl, her body was cold, shivering. No wonder, in this dark prison. "Come." He led her out into the light and closed the door. Her clothes could wait. More important now to warm and reassure her that she was safe. With him. He pulled a wing chair closer to the fire and pushed her down into it. Then he fetched the coverlet from the bed and wrapped it round her. "Better?"

Her beautiful eyes had adjusted to the light now. She nodded. "Thank you." Her voice was a thready whisper.

He poured a small brandy and pressed it into her hand. "Drink this. It will warm you and give you strength." He expected her to protest, but she did not. She nodded, tossed it down, and then began to cough uncontrollably. He saw that she was beautiful, and fragile, and vulnerable, all at the same time, and yet as brave as any soldier. One in a million.

"Oh, my darling girl," Robert burst out, "you must take care." Her coughing stopped. For a long moment, he simply held her close. Something had changed between them. But there was no time now to explore the strange new feelings that had engulfed him.

Being held in his arms was heavenly. Especially after so long in that dark prison. She had heard a commotion, and raised voices, but she had been unable to make out what was going on. She had been so very afraid for

Robert.

"Courage, my sweet. It is over. Your uncle has gone."

She rested her head against the hard strength of his body and closed her eyes. They were safe. For the moment.

"And now we must organise a wedding." He chuckled into her hair. "In some haste, I fear."

She looked anxiously up into his face. He would marry her for honour's sake, even though he did not love her. Did he feel trapped, resentful?

To her surprise, he was smiling warmly down at her, his gaze as gentle as a caress. A loving caress. "Oh," she breathed.

"Come, my sweet." He crossed to the little desk and pulled out a chair for her. "You have to write a letter. We need to gain time. We must give the hounds a false scent."

"Oh, yes, of course. I imagine you cannot organise a wedding overnight, even with a special licence."

"A special—" He threw back his head and laughed. "Oh, my darling girl, life with you will certainly be full of surprises. How old are you?"

She bristled. "Twenty, sir."

"And do you have your guardian's permission for this marriage you are about to enter into?"

Oh. She shook her head. She knew what was coming next.

"Precisely so. Sadly, this is not Verona with a Friar Lawrence conveniently to hand. This is England, and England's laws do not permit an under-age girl to consent to marriage. It is a weary road back to Scotland, but at least the days are long at this time of year, and the weather is set fair. I am only sorry that we shall have to use the services at Gretna rather than waiting for a minister of the kirk. But you shall have a proper wedding afterwards, I promise. In the kirk."

Isobel straightened her shoulders. The mere thought of spending days with Robert in the confines of a post chaise had her insides heating and melting. She tried not to dwell on that. There would be a time for desire. Later.

Especially if what she had seen in his eyes was love.

She forced herself to sit demurely at the desk.

After a moment's thought, Robert said, "We must turn you into a selfish, top-lofty young woman, I fear. It is the only way. Try this."

Isobel wrote at his dictation. *Annie, Pray tell my dear aunt that I beg her pardon for having left so abruptly, but I could not consent to marry a man so far beneath me, even to spare my papa. I shall stay with my friend Emma until Mr Craigie has withdrawn. Impress upon my dear aunt, pray, that my uncle must* not *come here after me. My kind hostess moves in the highest circles, but even she could not prevent the scandal that would result.*

"That will do, I think," he said. "And now you must write a covering note to Annie, so that—"

"Wait, Robert. This will *not* do. My uncle will soon discover that I am not at Lady Manson's house."

Robert shook his head. "Oh, ye of little faith." He picked up a clean quill pen and the water carafe. "Watch." He deftly placed a tiny drop of water on the word "Emma". The letters blurred and become quite illegible. To complete the deception, he dripped on other parts of the paper, too. "You wrote this in a mood of guilty resolution. Determined, but unable to hold back your tears."

He pulled out a fresh sheet. "And now the note to Annie."

Obediently, Isobel wrote at his dictation, instructing the maid to do everything possible to put her uncle off the scent, and then to travel to Scotland, with Grant.

"Two days' start should be enough," Robert said firmly, pulling her to her feet and into his embrace.

She could trust him. He would save them both. She gazed up into his beloved face, hoping, longing to see some sign that he might one day feel more than mere desire when she was in his arms.

What she saw there took her breath away.

He stroked her hair back from her temple with a sure, possessive hand. "You will be safe very soon, under the protection of my name. As my most beloved wife."

Her long sigh of delight was captured in his kiss, the kiss of a man who loves and beloved in return.

EPILOGUE

The Times, London, July 1800:
Lately, Major Robert Anstruther to Miss Isobel Lang Ritchie.

"WHAT DID YOUR FATHER MEAN, ROBERT? He said you had given him an ultimatum. And then he laughed. Is there some private joke between you?" She snuggled more closely into the crook of Robert's arm and slithered a hand over his naked stomach, ignoring his sharply indrawn breath.

He put his fingers over hers and held them still. "I cannot think when you do that, my love. If you want a coherent answer, you must behave." She sighed loudly. "Not for long, I promise." He dropped a kiss on the top of her ear.

Neither of them spoke. They simply relaxed into each other's embrace. They were married, and one flesh. Star-crossed no longer. Soon there would be another glorious joining. But that could wait a little while. Even waiting could be pleasurable.

He stroked her hair. "My father is not long for this world. He has had too many seizures. He confidently expects the next one to carry him off."

"Robert! You must not—"

"No, love. There can be no pretending. He does not wish it. He says he is ready to meet his maker. He means to put an end to the Ritchie-Anstruther feud."

She caught her breath. "Was it you who—?"

"I urged him to it, I admit. In the face of death, he sees that it is futile, and condemns the grandchildren he will not live to see. He spent his life pursuing that feud, and now he is equally determined to see it finished. He is not a man to cross, even now. And his mind is still sharp enough to have found a way."

"But how?"

"He is making a new will. He will leave a large legacy to Archibald Ritchie, with a dying man's wish that it be used to restore the Ritchies' standing in the world. In return, my father asks only that yours will bless the union of our two families, and care for his grandchildren." He touched a finger to Isobel's cheek and wiped away a stray tear. "I pray that your father will not refuse."

"He—" She stopped and thought hard. She should know her father well enough to be sure. "My father is stubborn, but he is an honourable man. I hope...I think he will feel bound to accept." She gazed up at her beloved husband through her tears. "If only your poor papa did not have to die to accomplish this. It seems so very sad..."

"Aye, and so it is. But he would not have you weep, my darling. He would have us celebrate life, and the love we have found together." He lifted her fingers and laid them on the very definite evidence of his need.

Isobel sighed in satisfaction and curled her hand round his flesh, tightening her grasp until he groaned, deep in his chest.

"You truly do know how to torment a man, Mrs Anstruther."

"Not *any* man, sir. Only the one man who showed me how very special love can be, when it is given and returned in equal measure." She slid her hand up his hard length, until he arched his neck with the exquisite agony of it. She squeezed again.

"That, madam, is quite enough of that." His voice was little more than a gasp. With a deft flick, he rolled her on to her back and settled into the cradle of her hips. "What I need now is all of you." He slid into her body in one long, glorious stroke and then stilled. "I have you now, my love.

"And tomorrow," he whispered into her ear, his mouth so close that his breath made her shiver deliciously, "I think I shall take you back to Caerlaverock. I shall make love to you there in the twilight, under the stars. My darling nymph shall be earthbound, for ever. We were so nearly star-crossed lovers. Let us show those old stones that twilight lovers can *live* for each other, too."

And then he kissed her, and it was as if the whole canopy of stars was enfolding them, and smiling down on their union.

THE END

DEAR READER
FROM JOANNA MAITLAND

I hope you have enjoyed reading about how Robert and Isobel manage to reach their happy ending, in spite of the centuries-old feud between their families. Their story has similarities with *Romeo and Juliet*, of course – and that is why I changed the title for this second edition – but I am glad to say that, unlike Shakespeare's sad star-crossed lovers, my Regency couple do *not* have to die in order to end the family feud. They enjoy many years of very happy marriage.

Their lives together are not without trials, however, as you'll discover if you read my full-length story, **Bride of the Solway**, set fifteen years later. There you'll meet Robert and Isobel again, supporting my new hero, Captain Ross Graham, an exiled Scot. Ross has returned to Dumfries to search for his lost family roots and to nurse a broken heart. He meets unexpected dangers, powerful opponents, and Cassandra, a lady in distress. Ross decides Cassie is definitely in need of rescuing. But spirited Cassie has ideas of her own. Sparks will fly!

Bride of the Solway is available as a digital download from most ebook outlets.

ABOUT THE AUTHOR

Joanna Maitland has published 13 Regency historicals with Harlequin Mills & Boon since 2000 and has sold well over a million copies around the world, with readers in countries as diverse as Japan and Brazil. She is now an independently published author. She is continuing to write Regencies, but also hopping over the hedge into lush new pastures, like medieval and time-slip. If there's history involved, Joanna is up for it!

Joanna is one of the founding partners of Libertà Books. She is also a proud and long-standing member of the Romantic Novelists' Association which recently honoured her by making her a Vice President of the Association.

For news, free stories and more, visit Joanna's new website at libertabooks.com where you can have your say on the blog, or maybe write a love letter to a favourite novel.

Intrigued? Have a look and see whether you would like to join in. Libertà often hosts writers you will know.

You can follow Joanna using her Twitter handle @JoannaMaitland or on Facebook www.facebook.com/libertabooks

HIS SILKEN SEDUCTION
A Regency Novella

Wounded. Abandoned. In the enemy's bed

He's Wellington's spy, trying to survive in war-torn France. He has a choice – duty, or desire.

She's his beautiful silk weaver. Day after day, her hands caress his battered flesh. Her touch is driving him wild.
But she's the enemy. She must not discover who he is. Surely she will betray him?

Will he dare to trust her
with his life, his mission, and his heart?

Read on for an extract

CHAPTER ONE

France, March 1815

THEY WERE COMING FOR HIM.

They had come out of nowhere. Five of them. And they had knives.

Ben started to run. What choice did he have? He was alone. No…no, Jack was about somewhere. Where? Ben couldn't see him, but he must be—

No time to think about that. It didn't matter anyway. Two against five was very poor odds, especially when the two were unarmed and the five were not. It was every man for himself.

Run, you idiot. The voice in his head was

insistent. *Faster! If they catch you, you're dead meat.*

Ben put on a spurt. He could do this. He could.

He must.

He was almost out of the old port area. Just another few yards to the end of the quay. There must be safety up ahead. Somewhere. Somewhere less dangerous. With civilised people. If only he could—

Pain ripped through him.

Then – only then – he heard the report. A shot. One of those blackguards had shot him. And he was falling. Falling...

His last thought was to wonder why the ball had hit him before he had even heard the shot.

And then he was floating. Surrounded by shifting dark mists that rolled and twisted into fantastical patterns and shapes. Bringing with them strange, sun-drenched scents.

Am I dead? He dragged in a desperately needed breath. And discovered how much it hurt. *If it hurts, I can't be dead, can I?*

He sucked in another breath. And a blinding light burst through the pain. He remembered. If he was injured, how could they continue with their mission? Their mission for Wellington was vital. Nothing else mattered. Nothing. He groaned out the precious words. "Mission. Wellington." As if, by speaking them aloud, he could make all right again. "Mission."

Those perfumes were swirling around him once more. This time, they swept him off to a hot sunny hillside, where he found himself lying on springy grass, gazing up at the sky through yellow puffs of mimosa flowers, drinking in scents of lavender and rosemary. But with his next breath, the dark shrouds closed in again, suffocating him and swallowing the sky.

He wanted to cry out, to fight against the blanketing mists, but he did not have the strength. Their long grey fingers stroked him into darkness, deep as a pit.

Even in the darkness, there was pain. Piercing, unbearable pain, like daggers in his flesh. Ben tried to move, to throw them off, somehow, anyhow, but the enveloping web was looped round and under him, tying him in a tangled thicket from which it seemed he would never break free. And always the daggers. The daggers. He groaned and thrashed his body from side to side. If he was not dead, he must fight. He must.

"Sleep now," said a soft voice. It was barely a murmur but it soothed. It must have been sent from heaven. An angel? Cool clean linen was laid on his forehead, as refreshing as joyful rain on dry earth. Ben felt the knots unravel as his bonds receded into the grey mist, defeated by the angel's hand.

If I can sleep, I cannot be dead. If I can sleep… If I can only sleep…

It was not sleep that came. It was torture. Suddenly, he was being tossed back and forth between giants. And they were rejoicing at his groans of pain. This was not heaven. This was hell, full of red-hot needles and tongues of fire. From this, there could be no escape. His angel had forsaken him.

He cried out.

And his angel returned. His fair-haired angel. Calling his name, through the whirling flames. He wanted to reach for her, but he was pinioned. He could not escape.

"French," the angel said sternly. "You must speak only French. No English. Only French."

He was in a French heaven. Or was it hell? But his angel spoke French and so he must do so, too. "No English," he croaked.

Which language had he spoken? He could not tell. He could not hear his own voice. The circling shrouds were sucking it away, swallowing his words, swallowing everything. Were they trying to suck out his soul?

He gave a great cry of anguish. But it could not save him. The pit was opening at his feet and he was falling. Down, down, down. Into blackness.

He must climb out of the pit. He must. If he could free his arms, he could climb. He could claw his way out of this blackness. He began to struggle against the invisible bonds that held him...

"Herr Benn."

It was his angel's voice. No, not hers. Another's. Another angel?

He struggled even harder to break free of the darkness. To reach her.

"Herr Benn, no! You will injure yourself. Wake up. Oh, pray, wake up."

A hand on his shoulder. Shaking him.

He was out of the pit. He could open his eyes. There was light. Bright, blinding light.

And his angel was still there, still there

behind the light, still speaking to him in that sweet, urgent voice.

"Herr Benn. Oh, Herr Benn, you are yourself again. Thank heaven. You were having such a nightmare and I could not wake you. Are you...are you well now?"

She was speaking French to him. And the room was spinning. Had he really been dreaming? The pit was not real? Nor the giants with their red-hot needles?

A hand stroked a cooling cloth across his brow. Then it brought a cup to his lips and helped him to drink. The prickle of sharp lemon on his tongue was no dream. He was alive. This was real.

He turned his head a fraction to search for his angel's face, hoping desperately that she, too, was real.

Everything was blurred. The light was too bright. In desperation, he screwed up his eyes against it, struggling to focus. There was... Yes, he could just make out a halo of fair curls filled with sunlight. And then, at last, a face.

He sighed out a long, thankful breath. His angel was still at his side. She was real.

And she was beautiful.

He did not know who she was, but all at once he understood the meaning of his dream. It was all true, even though it was a weird jumble of memories, interlaced with pain. He and Jack were on a spying mission for Wellington. They had been set upon by a gang of villains as they left Marseilles. And one of the assailants had had a gun.

"Did they shoot me?" he croaked, in French,

gazing pleadingly at his angel. He was hot and aching. Covered in sweat. And the pain was certainly real. It seemed to be worst on his right side. He began to reach with his left hand, to find out how badly he was wounded.

Soft fingers caught his hand and held it. "Do not distress yourself, Herr Benn," the angel said, frowning down at him. "Yes, you were shot, but the bullet is gone and the wound is clean. Pray do not claw at your bandages. Your shoulder will heal better if you rest." She pushed him gently back on to feather pillows and laid his hand firmly on the coverlet.

"I… Where am I?" He had not seen this girl before, had he? She looked familiar and yet she was not. He would not have forgotten such fragile beauty.

She smiled at him. The frown melted away, leaving her skin smooth as a peach. "You are in Lyons. You were brought here by your friend, Monsieur Jacques, and my sister, Marguerite Grolier. You are safe here, in our weaving house."

That was why she seemed familiar! The silk weaver was her sister. And he had seen the silk weaver in his dreams, had he not? Had she not admonished him to speak only French?

He was having difficulty working out what was real and what was fantasy. "Jacques is here? I need to speak to him." Jack would be able to explain everything. Jack would set Ben's topsy-turvy memories to rights. Unless… "Jacques? Did they shoot him, too?"

"Be easy, sir. Your friend came off with a whole skin. As did my sister. You were the

94

only casualty."

Ben sighed. What a relief. He said as much.

"For a German, you speak very good French, Herr Benn," she said, smiling broadly at him now. "You have very little accent."

Another piece of the puzzle slotted into place at her words. Of course. Since, unlike Jack, Ben could not speak French like a native, they had agreed that Ben would pretend to be a German. He had become Herr Christian Benn, while Jack had become Monsieur Louis Jacques, a *bourgeois* from Paris. Ben must remember to play his part. Was there anything else that he needed to remember? And beware of?

He must speak French. Only French. No English.

And he must find out the name of this fair-haired angel.

She offered him the cup again and he drank greedily. "Thank you," he said. "Thank you, Miss...er... Your pardon, ma'am. I'm afraid I do not know your name."

"It is Grolier, of course. Suzanne Grolier."

"Suzanne." He repeated it several times, relishing the taste of the syllables on his tongue. "It is a beautiful name. It suits you."

She was blushing. "You must not say such things," she said, flustered. She grabbed the cup and made a great show of gathering up the linen she had been using to bathe his face. Then she retreated towards the door.

"Please don't go," Ben said.

"I must. You need to rest."

"But I cannot rest if I do not have your

promise to return. Will you promise?"

Her blush was even deeper now, but after a moment she bit her lip and gave a tiny nod. "I will come back later to tend your wound. Provided you promise, in your turn, Herr Benn, to do everything I tell you to."

He frowned, puzzled. He was missing something important here.

She took a few steps forward so that she was standing at the end of the bed, looking gravely down at him. "You are an invalid. I am your nurse. A patient must obey his nurse or he will never get well." Suddenly, she smiled at him, a mischievous smile that lit up her delicate features. "You do want to get well, don't you, Herr Benn?"

If getting well would lose him that wonderful smile, he was not at all sure that he did.